P9-AQU-662

PORKER'S TAXI

PORKER'S TAXI

by Sven Nordqvist

Carolrhoda Books, Inc./Minneapolis

This edition first published 1992 by Carolrhoda Books, Inc.

Original edition published in 1991 by Opal under the title NASSES TAXI.
English language rights arranged by Kerstin Kvint Literary and Co-Production Agency, Stockholm, Sweden.

Library of Congress Cataloging-in-Publication Data

Nordqvist, Sven.
[Nasses Taxi. English]
Porker's Taxi / by Sven Nordqvist.
p. cm.
Translation of: Nasses Taxi
Summary: As he transports passengers uphill and downhill in his wheelbarrow, Porker makes an interesting discovery.
ISBN 0-87614-744-9
[1. Vehicles—Fiction.] I. Title.
PZ7.N7756Pp 1992
[E]—dc20 91-39496
CIP
AC

Manufactured in the United States of America

1 2 3 4 5 6 97 96 95 94 93 92

PORKER'S TAXI

One day when Porker is taking a walk, he finds something in the road. It has two sticks and a wheel and something blue underneath.

At first he doesn't know what it is, but then he sees that it is upside down, so he turns it over. When Porker grabs the two sticks, he realizes that this thing is something to run with. "How quickly it goes," he cries. "I can hardly keep up!"

Two rabbits come hopping along. "Hi, Porker. Is that your wheelbarrow?"

"Yes, I guess so. I was the one who found it," Porker answers. "See how fast it goes, this wheelbarrow? Fast as a shot, even though it only has one wheel."

"It's not that fast. We caught up with you in no time," the rabbits say.

"Yes, but there are two of you," Porker replies.

"Can we have a ride? We can pretend you're a taxi!" cry the rabbits.

"A taxi?" Porker stops. "What's a taxi?"

"It's a car that you pay to take you wherever you want to go." The rabbits jump into the wheelbarrow. "Take us to the green house as fast as you can!"

Porker turns the wheelbarrow around and pushes it in the direction of the green house. It's a bit uphill, and the going gets tough.

"Faster, Porker, faster!" The rabbits beg as they are tossed around.

"Sit still, otherwise it will tip over," Porker cries.

"No, sway more," the rabbits beg. "Drive crazy!"

"What do you mean, 'crazy'?"

"Steer us this way and that way and that way and this way, and hit all the water puddles!"

Porker drives crazy. The rabbits get tossed around even more, laughing all the way. "How heavy you are," Porker says. "Or else there are too many of you. I'm too tired to go on."

"What a weakling you are. You can't even drive two little rabbits." The rabbits pout as they hop off.

"I'm not weak," Porker thinks to himself. "I'm as strong as a bear. I *am* a bear! I'll show them."

The teacher comes walking by, carrying a suitcase.

"Taxi for hire!" cries Porker.

The teacher wants Porker to take him to the train station.

The station is back down the hill. Porker finds that it's easy to drive the taxi, even though the teacher is heavy.

"How fast we're going!" says the teacher delightedly. "Porker, would it be possible for you to drive a bit crazy? Swaying this way and that, so to speak?"

Porker drives crazy, through all the water puddles. The teacher bounces around in the wheelbarrow, clucking happily. Outside the station, Porker tips the wheelbarrow and the teacher falls out.

"I must say that was really an enjoyable journey," the teacher giggles. He gives Porker a coin and runs off to the train.

A woman standing at the station also wants to ride in the taxi. She has a white fur coat on.

"You're not a rabbit, are you?" Porker asks. "Rabbits are hard to push."

"No, thank goodness, I'm a fine lady," she answers primly.

The lady wants to go a little beyond the green house, so now it's uphill once again. Soon the trip gets too difficult for Porker. The wheelbarrow hits a bump in the road and tips over.

The lady falls out and is quite angry. Her coat has gotten dirty. "Ugh, what a terrible taxi! I'm going to report you to the taxi bureau!"

That doesn't bother Porker much because he doesn't know what the taxi bureau is. But he's sad that the lady is so angry.

Porker sits and thinks. Why is it that the rabbits and the lady were hard to drive, but the teacher was easy? The teacher was much bigger than the others. Could it be that furry things are heavier? It seems strange, but sometimes things aren't the way you think they should be.

Now along comes a man with a crate of apples that need to be taken to the store. The man asks Porker to take the apples in his taxi. The crate is big and heavy. Porker probably wouldn't even be able to lift it.

But driving the apples in the wheelbarrow is very easy. Soon Porker is at the store, and most of the apples are still in the crate. Porker gets to keep all the ones that have fallen out.

Porker thinks some more. The apples and the teacher were easy to drive, but the rabbits and the lady were difficult. So Porker writes on a piece of paper:

TAXI

I won't drive rabbits
or furry ladies.
I'd rather drive teachers
or apples.

He hangs the sign on the wheelbarrow.

A little old woman with a shopping bag comes out of the store. She wants to go home in Porker's taxi. Porker examines her. She has some fur on her hat. That's not good. But on the other hand, she's carrying apples in her bag. Apples are easy to drive. "It should be all right," Porker says, "but if it's too hard, you'll have to take off your hat."

The old woman climbs in, and Porker drives off. He's heading uphill again, and the wheelbarrow is rather difficult to push. Porker takes off the woman's hat and puts it on his own head, but it doesn't get any easier.

"Drive faster," shouts the old woman. "I must hurry home to make applesauce. And give me back my hat!"

"It's so hard," gasps Porker. "Apples are usually easier."

Finally they arrive. Porker is completely exhausted, but the woman doesn't pay him because she thinks he drove too slowly.

Porker looks at his sign and thinks some more. The big teacher was light, and the little old woman was heavy. He doesn't understand. Nothing seems to make sense.

The rabbits come by again. They want another ride in the taxi, but Porker says, "I won't drive rabbits anymore. They are too heavy."

"We're not heavy. We hardly weigh anything!"

"You were very heavy. You were much heavier than the teacher."

The rabbits think about this for a moment, and they begin to giggle.

"How silly you are, Porker. That's because you were driving us uphill. You drove the teacher downhill."

"What do you mean uphill and downhill? It was the same hill!"

"Oh, Porker!" The rabbits hop into the wheelbarrow. "Drive us to the store, and you'll see for yourself."

Porker hesitates. Then he takes a running start and pushes off. It's as easy as can be! The wheelbarrow is rolling along almost all by itself. Porker runs faster than he's ever run before.

Now he understands.

They reach the store in ten seconds, a new world record.

"That was no problem," Porker says. "It was the hill that was leaning the wrong way. I'll have to change my sign."

He writes instead:

TAXI—

downhill only

"That means I'll have only half as many customers. But that's OK, because then I won't have to run as much. Now *I* want to ride, and you two can push."

Porker sits in his taxi, and the rabbits push. "Take me to the raspberry bushes. Drive crazy!"

Author/illustrator **Sven Nordqvist** has enjoyed drawing since he was very young. But when he applied for admission to art school, he was turned down. Instead he became an architect and taught at The College of Architecture in Lund, Sweden.

Mr. Nordqvist returned to drawing eighteen years ago. He works as a free-lance artist and writer, specializing in children's books. His works radiate a sense of joy and playfulness that has attracted fans around the world.